For: James, Willow, Laurie and Wooster

Rockpool Children's Books
15 North Street
Marton
Warwickshire
CV23 9RJ

First published in Great Britain by Rockpool Children's Books Ltd. 2009
Text and Illustrations copyright © Heather Heyworth 2009
Heather Heyworth has asserted the moral rights
to be identified as the author and illustrator of this book.
© Rockpool Children's Books Ltd. 2009

Printed in China

rockpool
children's books

KNOWSLEY LIBRARY SERVICE

Knowsl@y Council

Please return this book on or before the date shown below

PROJECT LOAN FICTION

Heather Heyworth

Riding on an Elephant

Riding on an elephant, what do I see?

A tall giraffe
is looming, and
looking down at me.

Riding on an elephant,
what's in my view?

A pink and green chameleon,
changing now to blue.

Riding on an elephant, what do I see?

A roaring, growling lion,
scary as can be!

Riding
on an elephant,
what do I spy?

A chirpy, chatty monkey,
swinging way up high.

Riding on an elephant, what do I see?

A curly-wurly snake,
that slithers round my knee.

Riding on an elephant, what do I see?

A kangaroo on
holiday, hopping
round with glee.

Riding on an elephant, high above the ground,

I hear a bustling bumblebee,

a busy, buzzing sound.

Riding on an elephant, what do I see?

A squeaky,
cheeky mouse,
riding there for free.

Riding on an elephant, what do I see?

An emu
and his friend;
a tiny bouncing flea.

Looking back behind me,
what do I see?

Snake, giraffe and lion,
busy, buzzy bee,

Monkey, mouse and little friend,
tiny bouncing flea,
Chameleon, now turning red,
and hopping kangaroo.
And, hiding in the
undergrowth, is fluffy
emu too.

Sliding down an elephant, what do I see?

My jungle friends and gooey cake,
all here for birthday tea!

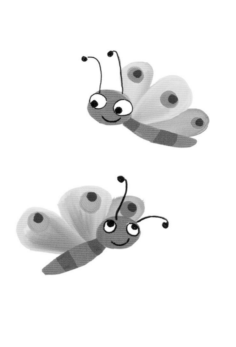